DOVER·THRIFT·EDITIONS

Uncle Vanya

ANTON CHEKHOV

DOVER PUBLICATIONS, INC.
Mineola, New York

DOVER THRIFT EDITIONS

GENERAL EDITOR: PAUL NEGRI

EDITOR OF THIS VOLUME: KATHY CASEY

Theatrical Rights

This Dover Thrift Edition may be used in its entirety, in adaptation, or in any other way for theatrical productions, professional and amateur, in the United States, without permission, fee, or acknowledgment. (This may not apply outside of the United States, as copyright conditions may vary.)

Bibliographical Note

This Dover edition, first published in 1998, is an unabridged republication of a standard edition. The Note was prepared specially for this edition.

Library of Congress Cataloging-in-Publication Data

Chekhov, Anton Pavlovich, 1860–1904.
  [Diadia Vania. English]
  Uncle Vanya / Anton Chekhov.
      p.   cm. — (Dover thrift editions)
  ISBN 0-486-40159-6
  I. Title.   II. Series.
PG3456.D5   1998
891.72'3—dc21   98-5424
                                                                          CIP

Manufactured in the United States of America
Dover Publications, Inc., 31 East 2nd Street, Mineola, N.Y. 11501

Note

Uncle Vanya is perhaps the most multi-faceted literary work of Anton Chekhov—who insisted, in his mature years, that his dramas were comedies, not tragedies. The play began life in 1888–89 as *The Wood Demon*, a lengthy four-act play that did not fully achieve its goal of juxtaposing semi-farcical and tragic perspectives on the relationships of middle-class, well-educated people on a country estate. It explores themes as diverse as male mid-life crisis; men's exploitation of the natural world and of women; the ruin that massive destruction of Russia's forests will cause; peasants' subjection to hunger, ill health, illiteracy, and ignorance; and hope for a joyful life after death as consolation for the miseries of earthly existence. Sometime between 1890 and 1896 Chekhov revised the play, cutting it extensively. The result was a haunting portrait of the sense of futility and wasted lives that burdened men and women enduring disappointments and frustrations amid rural tedium.

Anton Chekhov, the third of five children, was born in 1860 in the provincial town of Taganrog, on the Sea of Azov in south Russia. His strict father, who had been born a serf, tried to support the family by running a grocery store. As a boy, Anton had to work in his father's store and sing in the church choir his father conducted. After attending another local school, he studied for ten years at the town high school. He developed a strong dislike for the Greek and Latin classics and did not distinguish himself academically, but he was known for improvising humorous plays and for mimicking teachers.

In 1876 his bankrupt father moved the rest of the family to Moscow in hopes of making a fresh start. Anton remained in school, living alone and supporting himself by tutoring younger boys. After graduating in 1879, he joined his family in Moscow and began medical studies, earning his M.D. degree in 1884. (He practiced medicine only sporadically.) While a medical student, he was the main support of his mother and two younger siblings, as his father could obtain only low-paying employment, and his two older brothers, a journalist and an artist, provided little income to the family. Chekhov, using a pseudonym until 1888, became quite popular as a prolific writer of humorous sketches, which were published in several St. Petersburg journals and newspapers. After earning his medical degree, Chekhov began writing on tragic themes. By 1887 his serious writing began to displace the comic sketches and humorous stories, but humor remained an underlying element in much of his work. At the same time, his output diminished. He wrote only ten stories in 1888, compared with more than one hundred annually in the two preceding years.

In 1889 Chekhov's older brother Nikolai died of tuberculosis, the same disease that would end Anton's life prematurely. Some have seen a connection between his brother's death and the pessimism increasingly expressed in Chekhov's short stories at this time. During this period, critics complained that Chekhov did not express any social or political views in his work (something that was expected of Russian literary figures). Chekhov greatly valued both political and artistic freedom, but eschewed political involvement, and resented being told that his writing should provide political or social prescriptions.

Chekhov aided peasants decimated by illness during the severe famine of 1891–92. He then bought an estate fifty miles south of Moscow, where his parents and his younger sister lived with him. Earlier, Tolstoy's ideas of "the simple life" and nonresistance to evil had attracted him, but his short stories of this period show that he had rejected both concepts.

At its first performance in 1896, his four-act play *The Seagull* (a study of the clash of generations that was misnamed a comedy) almost was hissed off the stage at its first performance. However, it was presented successfully in December 1898 at the new Moscow Art Theater, and successful performances of *Uncle Vanya* followed. Unfortunately, in 1897 Chekhov had suffered a lung hemorrhage caused by tuberculosis, and he began spending his winters on the warm coasts of Crimea and the French Riviera. This prevented him from being present when his plays were being staged—just when his reputation as a dramatist was growing. He fell in love with a young actress, Olga Knipper, who performed in his plays, and they married in 1901, but the couple lived apart during the winters as she continued her career. *Three Sisters* was staged during the 1900–1901 season, and *The Cherry Orchard* in 1903–1904, but Chekhov, who described his plays as comedies, not tragedies, never thought that the director, Stanislavsky, achieved the light touch Chekhov craved in their presentation.

Chekhov died in 1904, physically depleted but still full of literary energy. His letters, published posthumously, were witty and lively, belying the belief of many that the great short story writer and playwright had had a pessimistic, dreary outlook on life.

Characters

Alexander Serebrakov, *a retired professor*
Helena, *his wife, twenty-seven years old*
Sonia, *his daughter by a former marriage*
Mme. Voitskaya, *widow of a privy councillor, and mother of Serebrakov's first wife*
Ivan (Vanya) Voitski, *her son*
Michael Astrov, *a doctor*
Ilia (Waffles) Telegin, *an impoverished landowner*
Marina, *an old nurse*
A Workman

The scene is Serebrakov's *country place.*

ACT I

A country house on a terrace. In front of it is a garden. In an avenue of trees, under an old poplar, stands a table set for tea, with a samovar, etc. Some benches and chairs stand near the table. On one of them is lying a guitar. A hammock is hung near the table. It is three o'clock in the afternoon of a cloudy day.

MARINA, *a quiet, gray-haired, little old woman, is sitting at the table knitting a stocking.*

ASTROV *is walking up and down near her.*

MARINA. [*Pouring some tea into a glass*] Take a little tea, my son.

ASTROV. [*Takes the glass from her unwillingly*] Somehow, I don't seem to want any.

MARINA. Then will you have a little vodka instead?

ASTROV. No, I don't drink vodka every day, and besides, it is too hot now. [*A pause*] Tell me, nurse, how long have we known each other?

MARINA. [*Thoughtfully*] Let me see, how long is it? Lord—help me to remember. You first came here, into our parts—let me think—when was it? Sonia's mother was still alive—it was two winters before she died; that was eleven years ago—[*thoughtfully*] perhaps more.

ASTROV. Have I changed much since then?

MARINA. Oh, yes. You were handsome and young then, and

now you are an old man and not handsome anymore. You drink, too.

ASTROV. Yes, ten years have made me another man. And why? Because I am overworked. Nurse, I am on my feet from dawn until dusk. I know no rest; at night I tremble under my blankets for fear of being dragged out to visit someone who is sick; I have toiled without repose or a day's freedom since I have known you; could I help growing old? And then, existence is tedious, anyway; it is a senseless, dirty business, this life, and goes heavily. Everyone about here is silly, and after living with them for two or three years one grows silly oneself. It is inevitable. [*Twisting his mustache*] See what a long mustache I have grown. A foolish, long mustache. Yes, I am as silly as the rest, nurse, but not as stupid; no, I have not grown stupid. Thank God, my brain is not addled yet, though my feelings have grown numb. I ask nothing, I need nothing, I love no one, unless it is yourself alone. [*He kisses her head*] I had a nurse just like you when I was a child.

MARINA. Don't you want a bite of something to eat?

ASTROV. No. During the third week of Lent I went to the epidemic at Malitskoi. It was eruptive typhoid. The peasants were all lying side by side in their huts, and the calves and pigs were running about the floor among the sick. Such dirt there was, and smoke! Unspeakable! I slaved among those people all day, not a crumb passed my lips, but when I got home there was still no rest for me; a switchman was carried in from the railroad; I laid him on the operating table and he went and died in my arms under chloroform, and then my feelings that should have been deadened awoke again, my conscience tortured me as if I had killed the man. I sat down and closed my eyes—like this— and thought: will our descendants two hundred years from now, for whom we are breaking the road, remember to give us a kind word? No, nurse, they will forget.

MARINA. Man is forgetful, but God remembers.

ASTROV. Thank you for that. You have spoken the truth.

Enter VOITSKI *from the house. He has been asleep after din-*

ner and looks rather disheveled. He sits down on the bench and straightens his collar.

VOITSKI. H'm. Yes. [*A pause*] Yes.

ASTROV. Have you been asleep?

VOITSKI. Yes, very much so. [*He yawns*] Ever since the professor and his wife have come, our daily life seems to have jumped the track. I sleep at the wrong time, drink wine, and eat all sorts of messes for luncheon and dinner. It isn't wholesome. Sonia and I used to work together and never had an idle moment, but now Sonia works alone and I only eat and drink and sleep. Something is wrong.

MARINA. [*Shaking her head*] Such a confusion in the house! The professor gets up at twelve, the samovar is kept boiling all the morning, and everything has to wait for him. Before they came we used to have dinner at one o'clock, like everybody else, but now we have it at seven. The professor sits up all night writing and reading, and suddenly, at two o'clock, there goes the bell! Heavens, what is that? The professor wants some tea! Wake the servants, light the samovar! Lord, what disorder!

ASTROV. Will they be here long?

VOITSKI. A hundred years! The professor has decided to make his home here.

MARINA. Look at this now! The samovar has been on the table for two hours, and they are all out walking!

VOITSKI. All right, don't get excited; here they come.

Voices are heard approaching. SEREBRAKOV, HELENA, SONIA, *and* TELEGIN *come in from the depths of the garden, returning from their walk.*

SEREBRAKOV. Superb! Superb! What beautiful views!

TELEGIN. They are wonderful, your Excellency.

SONIA. Tomorrow we shall go into the woods, shall we, Papa?

VOITSKI. Ladies and gentlemen, tea is ready.

SEREBRAKOV. Won't you please be good enough to send my tea into the library? I still have some work to finish.

SONIA. I am sure you will love the woods.

HELENA, SEREBRAKOV, *and* SONIA *go into the house.*
TELEGIN *sits down at the table beside* MARINA.

VOITSKI.   There goes our learned scholar on a hot, sultry day like this, in his overcoat and galoshes and carrying an umbrella!

ASTROV.   He is trying to take good care of his health.

VOITSKI.   How lovely she is! How lovely! I have never in my life seen a more beautiful woman.

TELEGIN.   Do you know, Marina, that as I walk in the fields or in the shady garden, as I look at this table here, my heart swells with unbounded happiness. The weather is enchanting, the birds are singing, we are all living in peace and contentment—what more could the soul desire?

[*Takes a glass of tea.*

VOITSKI.   [*Dreaming*] Such eyes—a glorious woman!

ASTROV.   Come, Ivan, tell us something.

VOITSKI.   [*Indolently*] What shall I tell you?

ASTROV.   Haven't you any news for us?

VOITSKI.   No, it is all stale. I am just the same as usual, or perhaps worse, because I have become lazy. I don't do anything now but croak like an old raven. My mother, the old magpie, is still chattering about the emancipation of woman, with one eye on her grave and the other on her learned books, in which she is always looking for the dawn of a new life.

ASTROV.   And the professor?

VOITSKI.   The professor sits in his library from morning until night, as usual:

> Straining the mind, wrinkling the brow,
> We write, write, write,
> Without respite
> Or hope of praise in the future or now.

Poor paper! He ought to write his autobiography; he would make a really splendid subject for a book! Imagine it, the life of a retired professor, as stale as a piece of hardtack, tortured by gout, headaches, and rheumatism, his liver bursting with jealousy and envy, living on the estate of his first wife, though he hates it, because he can't afford to live in town. He is everlastingly whining about his hard lot, though, as a matter of fact, he is extraordinarily lucky. He is the son of a common deacon and has attained the professor's chair, become the son-in-law of a senator, is called "your Excellency," and so on. But I'll tell you something; the man has been writing on art for twenty-five years, and he doesn't know the very first thing about it. For twenty-five years he has been chewing on other men's thoughts about realism, naturalism, and all such foolishness; for twenty-five years he has been reading and writing things that clever men have long known and stupid ones are not interested in; for twenty-five years he has been making his imaginary mountains out of molehills. And just think of the man's self-conceit and presumption all this time! For twenty-five years he has been masquerading in false clothes and has now retired, absolutely unknown to any living soul; and yet see him stalking across the earth like a demigod!

ASTROV. I believe you envy him.

VOITSKI. Yes, I do. Look at the success he has had with women! Don Juan himself was not more favored. His first wife, who was my sister, was a beautiful, gentle being, as pure as the blue heaven there above us, noble, great-hearted, with more admirers than he has pupils, and she loved him as only beings of angelic purity can love those who are as pure and beautiful as themselves. His mother-in-law, my mother, adores him to this day, and he still inspires a sort of worshipful awe in her. His second wife is, as you see, a brilliant beauty; she married him in his old age and has surrendered all the glory of her beauty and freedom to him. Why? What for?

ASTROV. Is she faithful to him?

VOITSKI. Yes, unfortunately she is.

ASTROV. Why "unfortunately"?

VOITSKI. Because such fidelity is false and unnatural, root and branch. It sounds well, but there is no logic in it. It is thought immoral for a woman to deceive an old husband whom she hates, but quite moral for her to strangle her poor youth in her breast and banish every vital desire from her heart.

TELEGIN.   [*In a tearful voice*] Vanya, I don't like to hear you talk so. Listen, Vanya; everyone who betrays husband or wife is faithless, and could also betray his country.

VOITSKI.   [*Crossly*] Turn off the tap, Waffles.

TELEGIN.   No, allow me, Vanya. My wife ran away with a lover on the day after our wedding, because my exterior was unprepossessing. I have never failed in my duty since then. I love her and am true to her to this day. I help her all I can and have given my fortune to educate the daughter of herself and her lover. I have forfeited my happiness, but I have kept my pride. And she? Her youth has fled, her beauty has faded according to the laws of nature, and her lover is dead. What has she kept?

> HELENA *and* SONIA *come in; after them comes* MME. VOITSKAYA *carrying a book. She sits down and begins to read. Someone hands her a glass of tea, which she drinks without looking up.*

SONIA.   [*Hurriedly, to the nurse*] There are some peasants waiting out there. Go and see what they want. I shall pour the tea.

> [*Pours out some glasses of tea.*

> MARINA *goes out.* HELENA *takes a glass and sits drinking in the hammock.*

ASTROV.   I have come to see your husband. You wrote me that he had rheumatism and I know not what else, and that he was very ill, but he appears to be as lively as a cricket.

HELENA.   He had a fit of the blues yesterday evening and complained of pains in his legs, but he seems all right again today.

ASTROV.   And I galloped over here twenty miles at breakneck speed! No matter, though, it is not the first time. Once here, however, I am going to stay until tomorrow, and at any rate sleep *quantum satis*.

SONIA.   Oh, splendid! You so seldom spend the night with us. Have you had dinner yet?

ASTROV.   No.

SONIA.   Good. So you will have it with us. We dine at seven now. [*Drinks her tea*] This tea is cold!

TELEGIN.   Yes, the samovar has grown cold.

HELENA.   Don't mind, Monsieur Ivan, we will drink cold tea, then.

TELEGIN.   I beg your pardon, my name is not Ivan, but Ilia, ma'am—Ilia Telegin, or Waffles, as I am sometimes called on account of my pockmarked face. I am Sonia's godfather, and his Excellency, your husband, knows me very well. I now live with you, ma'am, on this estate, and perhaps you will be so good as to notice that I dine with you every day.

SONIA.   He is our great help, our right-hand man. [*Tenderly*] Dear godfather, let me pour you some tea.

MME. VOITSKAYA.   Oh! Oh!

SONIA.   What is it, grandmother?

MME. VOITSKAYA.   I forgot to tell Alexander—I have lost my memory—I received a letter today from Paul Alexevitch in Kharkov. He has sent me a new pamphlet.

ASTROV.   Is it interesting?

MME. VOITSKAYA.   Yes, but strange. He refutes the very theories which he defended seven years ago. It is appalling!

VOITSKI.   There is nothing appalling about it. Drink your tea, Mamma.

MME. VOITSKAYA.   It seems you never want to listen to what I have to say. Pardon me, Jean, but you have changed so in the last year that I hardly know you. You used to be a man of settled convictions and had an illuminating personality——

VOITSKI.   Oh, yes. I had an illuminating personality, which illuminated no one. [*A pause*] I had an illuminating personality! You couldn't say anything more biting. I am forty-seven years old. Until last year I endeavored, as you do now, to blind my eyes by your pedantry to the truths of life. But now— Oh, if you only knew! If you knew how I lie awake at night, heartsick and angry, to think how stupidly I have wasted my time when I might have been winning from life everything which my old age now forbids.

SONIA. Uncle Vanya, how dreary!

MME. VOITSKAYA. [*To her son*] You speak as if your former convictions were somehow to blame, but you yourself, not they, were at fault. You have forgotten that a conviction, in itself, is nothing but a dead letter. You should have done something.

VOITSKI. Done something! Not every man is capable of being a writer *perpetuum mobile* like your Herr Professor.

MME. VOITSKAYA. What do you mean by that?

SONIA. [*Imploringly*] Mother! Uncle Vanya! I entreat you!

VOITSKI. I am silent. I apologize and am silent.

[*A pause.*

HELENA. What a fine day! Not too hot.

[*A pause.*

VOITSKI. A fine day to hang oneself.

TELEGIN *tunes the guitar.* MARINA *appears near the house, calling the chickens.*

MARINA. Chick, chick, chick!

SONIA. What did the peasants want, nurse?

MARINA. The same old thing, the same old nonsense. Chick, chick, chick!

SONIA. Why are you calling the chickens?

MARINA. The speckled hen has disappeared with her chicks. I am afraid the crows have got her.

TELEGIN *plays a polka. All listen in silence. Enter a* WORKMAN.

WORKMAN. Is the doctor here? [*To Astrov*] Excuse me, sir, but I have been sent to fetch you.

ASTROV. Where are you from?

WORKMAN. The factory.

ASTROV. [*Annoyed*] Thank you. There is nothing for it, then, but to go. [*Looking around him for his cap*] Damn it, this is annoying!

SONIA. Yes, it is too bad, really. You must come back to dinner from the factory.

ASTROV. No, I won't be able to do that. It will be too late. Now where, where— [*To* WORKMAN] Look here, my man, get me a glass of vodka, will you? [WORKMAN *goes out*] Where— where— [*Finds his cap*] One of the characters in Ostrov's plays is a man with a long mustache and short wits, like me. However, let me bid you good-bye, ladies and gentlemen. [*To* HELENA] I would be really delighted if you would come to see me someday with Miss Sonia. My estate is small, but if you are interested in such things I would like to show you a nursery and seedbed whose like you will not find within a thousand miles of here. My place is surrounded by government forests. The forester is old and always ailing, so I superintend almost all the work myself.

HELENA. I have always heard that you were very fond of the woods. Of course one can do a great deal of good by helping to preserve them, but does not that work interfere with your real calling?

ASTROV. God alone knows what a man's real calling is.

HELENA. And do you find it interesting?

ASTROV. Yes, very.

VOITSKI. [*Sarcastically*] Oh, extremely!

HELENA. You are still young, not over thirty-six or seven, I should say, and I suspect that the woods do not interest you as much as you say they do. I should think you would find them monotonous.

SONIA. No, the work is thrilling. Dr. Astrov watches over the old woods and sets out new plantations every year, and he has already received a diploma and a bronze medal. If you will listen to what he can tell you, you will agree with him entirely. He says that forests are the ornaments of the earth, that they teach mankind to understand beauty and attune his mind to lofty sentiments. Forests temper a stern climate, and in countries where the climate is milder, less strength is wasted in the battle with nature, and the people are kind and gentle. The inhabitants of such countries are handsome, tractable, sensitive, graceful in speech and gesture. Their philosophy is joyous, art and science blossom

among them, their treatment of women is full of exquisite nobil-
ity——

VOITSKI.   [*Laughing*] Bravo! Bravo! All that is very pretty, but
it is also unconvincing. [*To* ASTROV] So, my friend, you must let
me go on burning firewood in my stoves and building my sheds
of planks.

ASTROV.   You can burn peat in your stoves and build your
sheds of stone. Oh, I don't object, of course, to cutting wood
from necessity, but why destroy the forests? The woods of Russia
are trembling under the blows of the axe. Millions of trees have
perished. The homes of the wild animals and birds have been
desolated; the rivers are shrinking, and many beautiful land-
scapes are gone forever. And why? Because men are too lazy and
stupid to stoop down and pick up their fuel from the ground. [*To*
HELENA] Am I not right, Madame? Who but a stupid barbarian
could burn so much beauty in his stove and destroy that which
he cannot make? Man is endowed with reason and the power to
create, so that he may increase that which has been given him,
but until now he has not created, but demolished. The forests are
disappearing, the rivers are running dry, the game is extermi-
nated, the climate is spoiled, and the earth becomes poorer and
uglier every day. [*To* VOITSKI] I read irony in your eye; you do not
take what I am saying seriously, and—and—after all, it may very
well be nonsense. But when I pass peasant forests that I have pre-
served from the axe, or hear the rustling of the young plantations
set out with my own hands, I feel as if I had had some small share
in improving the climate, and that if mankind is happy a thousand years from now I will have been a little bit responsible for
their happiness. When I plant a little birch tree and then see it
budding into young green and swaying in the wind, my heart
swells with pride and I— [*Sees the* WORKMAN, *who is bringing
him a glass of vodka on a tray*] however— [*He drinks*] I must be
off. Probably it is all nonsense, anyway. Good-bye.

> *He goes toward the house.* SONIA *takes his arm and goes with
> him.*

SONIA.   When are you coming to see us again?
ASTROV.   I can't say.
SONIA.   In a month?

ASTROV *and* SONIA *go into the house.* HELENA *and* VOITSKI
walk over to the terrace.

HELENA.   You have behaved shockingly again. Ivan, what
sense was there in teasing your mother and talking about *perpetuum mobile*? And at breakfast you quarreled with Alexander
again. Really, your behavior is too petty.

VOITSKI.   But if I hate him?

HELENA.   You hate Alexander without reason; he is like
everyone else, and no worse than you are.

VOITSKI.   If you could only see your face, your gestures! Oh,
how tedious your life must be.

HELENA.   It is tedious, yes, and dreary! You all abuse my husband and look on me with compassion; you think, "Poor woman,
she is married to an old man." How well I understand your compassion! As Astrov said just now, see how you thoughtlessly destroy the forests, so that there will soon be none left. So you also
destroy mankind, and soon fidelity and purity and self-sacrifice
will have vanished with the woods. Why cannot you look calmly
at a woman unless she is yours? Because, the doctor was right,
you are all possessed by a devil of destruction; you have no mercy
on the woods or the birds or on women or on one another.

VOITSKI.   I don't like your philosophy.

HELENA.   That doctor has a sensitive, weary face—an interesting face. Sonia evidently likes him, and she is in love with
him, and I can understand it. This is the third time he has been
here since I have come, and I have not had a real talk with him
yet or made much of him. He thinks I am disagreeable. Do you
know, Ivan, the reason you and I are such friends? I think it is because we are both lonely and unfortunate. Yes, unfortunate.
Don't look at me in that way, I don't like it.

VOITSKI.   How can I look at you otherwise when I love you?
You are my joy, my life, and my youth. I know that my chances

of being loved in return are infinitely small, do not exist, but I ask nothing of you. Only let me look at you, listen to your voice——

HELENA.   Hush, someone will overhear you.

                                        [*They go toward the house.*

VOITSKI.   [*Following her*] Let me speak to you of my love, do not drive me away, and this alone will be my greatest happiness!

HELENA.   Ah! This is agony!

> TELEGIN *strikes the strings of his guitar and plays a polka.* MME. VOITSKAYA *writes something on the leaves of her pamphlet.*

> *The curtain falls.*

ACT II

The dining room of SEREBRAKOV's *house. It is night. The tapping
of the* WATCHMAN's *rattle is heard in the garden.*
SEREBRAKOV *is dozing in an armchair by an open window
and* HELENA *is sitting beside him, also half asleep.*

SEREBRAKOV. [*Rousing himself*] Who is here? Is it you,
Sonia?
HELENA.   It is I.
SEREBRAKOV.   Oh, it is you, Nelly. This pain is intolerable.
HELENA.   Your shawl has slipped down. [*She wraps up his
legs in the shawl*] Let me shut the window.
SEREBRAKOV.   No, leave it open; I am suffocating. I dreamed
just now that my left leg belonged to someone else, and it hurt so
that I woke. I don't believe this is gout, it is more like rheuma-
tism. What time is it?
HELENA.   Half past twelve.

[*A pause.*

SEREBRAKOV.   I want you to look for Batushka's works in the
library tomorrow. I think we have him.
HELENA.   What is that?
SEREBRAKOV.   Look for Batushka tomorrow morning; we
used to have him, I remember. Why do I find it so hard to
breathe?
HELENA.   You are tired; this is the second night you have had
no sleep.
SEREBRAKOV.   They say that Turgenev got angina of the heart

13

from gout. I am afraid I am getting angina too. Oh, damn this horrible, accursed old age! Ever since I have been old I have been hateful to myself, and I am sure, hateful to you all as well.

HELENA.   You speak as if we were to blame for your being old.

SEREBRAKOV.   I am more hateful to you than to anyone.

HELENA *gets up and walks away from him, sitting down at a distance.*

SEREBRAKOV.   You are quite right, of course. I am not an idiot; I can understand you. You are young and healthy and beautiful, and longing for life, and I am an old dotard, almost a dead man already. Don't I know it? Of course I see that it is foolish for me to live so long, but wait! I shall soon set you all free. My life cannot drag on much longer.

HELENA.   You are overtaxing my powers of endurance. Be quiet, for God's sake!

SEREBRAKOV.   It appears that, thanks to me, everybody's power of endurance is being overtaxed; everybody is miserable, only I am blissfully triumphant. Oh, yes, of course!

HELENA.   Be quiet! You are torturing me.

SEREBRAKOV.   I torture everybody. Of course.

HELENA.   [*Weeping*] This is unbearable! Tell me, what is it you want me to do?

SEREBRAKOV.   Nothing.

HELENA.   Then be quiet, please.

SEREBRAKOV.   It is funny that everybody listens to Ivan and his old idiot of a mother, but the moment I open my lips you all begin to feel ill-treated. You can't even stand the sound of my voice. Even if I am hateful, even if I am a selfish tyrant, haven't I the right to be one at my age? Haven't I deserved it? Haven't I, I ask you, the right to be respected, now that I am old?

HELENA.   No one is disputing your rights. [*The window slams in the wind*] The wind is rising, I must shut the window. [*She shuts it*] We shall have rain in a moment. Your rights have never been questioned by anybody.

The WATCHMAN *in the garden sounds his rattle.*

SEREBRAKOV.   I have spent my life working in the interests of learning. I am used to my library and the lecture hall and to the esteem and admiration of my colleagues. Now I suddenly find myself plunged in this wilderness, condemned to see the same stupid people from morning until night and listen to their futile conversation. I want to live; I long for success and fame and the stir of the world, and here I am in exile! Oh, it is dreadful to spend every moment grieving for the lost past, to see the success of others and sit here with nothing to do but to fear death. I cannot stand it! It is more than I can bear. And you will not even forgive me for being old!

HELENA.   Wait, have patience; I shall be old myself in four or five years.

SONIA *comes in.*

SONIA.   Father, you sent for Dr. Astrov, and now when he comes you refuse to see him. It is not nice to give a man so much trouble for nothing.

SEREBRAKOV.   What do I care about your Astrov? He understands medicine about as well as I understand astronomy.

SONIA.   We can't send for the whole medical faculty, can we, to treat your gout?

SEREBRAKOV.   I won't talk to that madman!

SONIA.   Do as you please. It's all the same to me.

[She sits down.

SEREBRAKOV.   What time is it?

HELENA.   One o'clock.

SEREBRAKOV.   It is stifling in here. Sonia, hand me that bottle on the table.

SONIA.   Here it is.

[She hands him a bottle of medicine.

SEREBRAKOV.   [*Crossly*] No, not that one! Can't you understand me? Can't I ask you to do a thing?

SONIA.   Please don't be captious with me. Some people may like it, but you must spare me, if you please, because I don't.

Besides, I haven't the time; we are cutting the hay tomorrow and I must get up early.

> VOITSKI *comes in dressed in a long gown and carrying a candle.*

VOITSKI. A thunderstorm is coming up. [*The lightning flashes*] There it is! Go to bed, Helena and Sonia. I have come to take your place.

SEREBRAKOV. [*Frightened*] No, no, no! Don't leave me alone with him! Oh, don't. He will begin to lecture me.

VOITSKI. But you must give them a little rest. They have not slept for two nights.

SEREBRAKOV. Then let them go to bed, but you go away too! Thank you. I implore you to go. For the sake of our former friendship do not protest against going. We will talk some other time——

VOITSKI. Our former friendship! Our former——

SONIA. Hush, Uncle Vanya!

SEREBRAKOV. [*To his wife*] My darling, don't leave me alone with him. He will begin to lecture me.

VOITSKI. This is ridiculous.

> MARINA *comes in carrying a candle.*

SONIA. You must go to bed, nurse, it is late.

MARINA. I haven't cleared away the tea things. Can't go to bed yet.

SEREBRAKOV. No one can go to bed. They are all worn out, only I enjoy perfect happiness.

MARINA. [*Goes up to* SEREBRAKOV *and speaks tenderly*] What's the matter, master? Does it hurt? My own legs are aching too, oh, so badly. [*Arranges his shawl about his legs*] You have had this illness such a long time. Sonia's dead mother used to stay awake with you too, and wear herself out for you. She loved you dearly. [*A pause*] Old people want to be pitied as much as young ones, but nobody cares about them somehow. [*She kisses* SEREBRAKOV's *shoulder*] Come, master, let me give you some linden tea and warm your poor feet for you. I shall pray to God for you.

SEREBRAKOV. [*Touched*] Let us go, Marina.

MARINA. My own feet are aching so badly, oh, so badly! [*She and* SONIA *lead* SEREBRAKOV *out*] Sonia's mother used to wear herself out with sorrow and weeping. You were still little and foolish then, Sonia. Come, come, master.

SEREBRAKOV, SONIA *and* MARINA *go out.*

HELENA. I am absolutely exhausted by him, and can hardly stand.

VOITSKI. You are exhausted by him, and I am exhausted by my own self. I have not slept for three nights.

HELENA. Something is wrong in this house. Your mother hates everything but her pamphlets and the professor; the professor is vexed, he won't trust me, and fears you; Sonia is angry with her father, and with me, and hasn't spoken to me for two weeks; I am at the end of my strength, and have come near bursting into tears at least twenty times today. Something is wrong in this house.

VOITSKI. Leave speculating alone.

HELENA. You are cultured and intelligent, Ivan, and you surely understand that the world is not destroyed by villains and conflagrations, but by hate and malice and all this spiteful tattling. It is your duty to make peace, and not to growl at everything.

VOITSKI. Help me first to make peace with myself. My darling!

[*Seizes her hand.*

HELENA. Let go! [*She drags her hand away*] Go away!

VOITSKI. Soon the rain will be over, and all nature will sigh and awake refreshed. Only I am not refreshed by the storm. Day and night the thought haunts me like a fiend, that my life is lost forever. My past does not count, because I frittered it away on trifles, and the present has so terribly miscarried! What shall I do with my life and my love? What is to become of them? This wonderful feeling of mine will be wasted and lost as a ray of sunlight is lost that falls into a dark chasm, and my life will go with it.

HELENA. I am, as it were, benumbed when you speak to me of your love, and I don't know how to answer you. Forgive me, I have nothing to say to you. [*She tries to go out*] Good night!

VOITSKI. [*Barring the way*] If you only knew how I am tortured by the thought that beside me in this house is another life that is being lost forever—it is yours! What are you waiting for? What accursed philosophy stands in your way? Oh, understand, understand——

HELENA. [*Looking at him intently*] Ivan, you are drunk!

VOITSKI. Perhaps. Perhaps.

HELENA. Where is the doctor?

VOITSKI. In there, spending the night with me. Perhaps I am drunk, perhaps I am; nothing is impossible.

HELENA. Have you just been drinking together? Why do you do that?

VOITSKI. Because in that way I get a taste of life. Let me do it, Helena!

HELENA. You never used to drink, and you never used to talk so much. Go to bed, I am tired of you.

VOITSKI. [*Falling on his knees before her*] My sweetheart, my beautiful one——

HELENA. [*Angrily*] Leave me alone! Really, this has become too disagreeable.

HELENA *goes out. A pause.*

VOITSKI. [*Alone*] She is gone! I met her first ten years ago, at her sister's house, when she was seventeen and I was thirty-seven. Why did I not fall in love with her then and propose to her? It would have been so easy! And now she would have been my wife. Yes, we would both have been waked tonight by the thunderstorm, and she would have been frightened, but I would have held her in my arms and whispered: "Don't be afraid! I am here." Oh, enchanting dream, so sweet that I laugh to think of it. [*He laughs*] But my God! My head reels! Why am I so old? Why

won't she understand me? I hate all that rhetoric of hers, that
morality of indolence, that absurd talk about the destruction of
the world— [A *pause*] Oh, how I have been deceived! For years
I have worshipped that miserable gout-ridden professor. Sonia
and I have squeezed this estate dry for his sake. We have bartered
our butter and curds and peas like misers, and have never kept a
morsel for ourselves, so that we could scrape enough pennies together to send to him. I was proud of him and of his learning; I
received all his words and writings as inspired, and now? Now he
has retired, and what is the total of his life? A blank! He is absolutely unknown, and his fame has burst like a soap bubble. I
have been deceived; I see that now, basely deceived.

> ASTROV *comes in. He has his coat on, but is without his
> waistcoat or collar, and is slightly drunk.* TELEGIN *follows
> him, carrying a guitar.*

ASTROV.   Play!
TELEGIN.   But everyone is asleep.
ASTROV.   Play!

> TELEGIN *begins to play softly.*

ASTROV.   Are you alone here? No women about?
                                    [*Sings with his arms akimbo.*

> The hut is cold, the fire is dead;
> Where shall the master lay his head?

The thunderstorm woke me. It was a heavy shower. What time is
it?
VOITSKI.   The devil only knows.
ASTROV.   I thought I heard Helena's voice.
VOITSKI.   She was here a moment ago.
ASTROV.   What a beautiful woman! [*Looking at the medicine
bottles on the table*] Medicine, is it? What a variety we have; prescriptions from Moscow, from Kharkov, from Tula! Why, he has
been pestering all the towns of Russia with his gout! Is he ill, or
simply shamming?

VOITSKI.   He is really ill.

ASTROV.   What is the matter with you tonight? You seem sad. Is it because you are sorry for the professor?

VOITSKI.   Leave me alone.

ASTROV.   Or in love with the professor's wife?

VOITSKI.   She is my friend.

ASTROV.   Already?

VOITSKI.   What do you mean by "already"?

ASTROV.   A woman can only become a man's friend after having first been his acquaintance and then his beloved—then she becomes his friend.

VOITSKI.   What vulgar philosophy!

ASTROV.   What do you mean? Yes, I must confess I am getting vulgar, but then, you see, I am drunk. I usually only drink like this once a month. At such times my audacity and temerity know no bounds. I feel capable of anything. I attempt the most difficult operations and do them magnificently. The most brilliant plans for the future take shape in my head. I am no longer a poor fool of a doctor, but mankind's greatest benefactor. I evolve my own system of philosophy and all of you seem to crawl at my feet like so many insects or microbes. [*To* TELEGIN] Play, Waffles!

TELEGIN.   My dear boy, I would with all my heart, but do listen to reason; everybody in the house is asleep.

ASTROV.   Play!

TELEGIN *plays softly.*

ASTROV.   I want a drink. Come, we still have some brandy left. And then, as soon as it is day, you will come home with me.

[*He sees* SONIA, *who comes in at that moment.*

ASTROV.   I beg your pardon, I have no collar on.

[*He goes out quickly, followed by* TELEGIN.

SONIA.   Uncle Vanya, you and the doctor have been drinking! The good fellows have been getting together! It is all very well for him, he has always done it, but why do you follow his example? It looks dreadfully at your age.

VOITSKI.   Age has nothing to do with it. When real life is wanting one must create an illusion. It is better than nothing.

SONIA.   Our hay is all cut and rotting in these daily rains, and here you are busy creating illusions! You have given up the farm altogether. I have done all the work alone until I am at the end of my strength— [*Frightened*] Uncle! Your eyes are full of tears!

VOITSKI.   Tears? Nonsense, there are no tears in my eyes. You looked at me then just as your dead mother used to, my darling— [*He eagerly kisses her face and hands*] My sister, my dearest sister, where are you now? Ah, if you only knew, if you only knew!

SONIA.   If she only knew what, Uncle?

VOITSKI.   My heart is bursting. It is awful. No matter, though. I must go.

[*He goes out.*

SONIA.   [*Knocks at the door*] Dr. Astrov! Are you awake? Please come here for a minute.

ASTROV.   [*Behind the door*] In a moment.

> He appears in a few seconds. He has put on his collar and
> waistcoat.

ASTROV.   What do you want?

SONIA.   Drink as much as you please yourself, if you don't find it revolting, but I implore you not to let my uncle do it. It is bad for him.

ASTROV.   Very well; we won't drink anymore. I am going home at once. That is settled. It will be dawn by the time the horses are harnessed.

SONIA.   It is still raining; wait until morning.

ASTROV.   The storm is blowing over. This is only the edge of it. I must go. And please don't ask me to come and see your father anymore. I tell him he has gout, and he says it is rheumatism. I tell him to lie down, and he sits up. Today he refused to see me at all.

SONIA.   He has been spoiled. [*She looks in the sideboard*] Won't you have a bite to eat?

ASTROV.   Yes, please. I believe I will.

SONIA.   I love to eat at night. I am sure we shall find something in here. They say that he has made a great many conquests in his life, and that the women have spoiled him. Here is some cheese for you.

[*They stand eating by the sideboard.*

ASTROV.   I haven't eaten anything today. Your father has a very difficult nature. [*He takes a bottle out of the sideboard*] May I? [*He pours himself a glass of vodka*] We are alone here, and I can speak frankly: Do you know, I could not stand living in this house for even a month? This atmosphere would stifle me. There is your father, entirely absorbed in his books, and his gout; there is your Uncle Vanya with his hypochondria, your grandmother, and finally, your stepmother——

SONIA.   What about her?

ASTROV.   A human being should be entirely beautiful: the face, the clothes, the mind, the thoughts. Your stepmother is, of course, beautiful to look at, but don't you see? She does nothing but sleep and eat and walk and bewitch us, and that is all. She has no responsibilities, everything is done for her—am I not right? And an idle life can never be a pure one. [*A pause*] However, I may be judging her too severely. Like your Uncle Vanya, I am discontented, and so we are both grumblers.

SONIA.   Aren't you satisfied with life?

ASTROV.   I like life as life, but I hate and despise it in a little Russian country village, and as far as my own personal life goes— by heaven! There is absolutely no redeeming feature about it. Haven't you noticed if you are riding through a dark wood at night and see a little light shining ahead, how you forget your fatigue and the darkness and the sharp twigs that whip your face? I work, that you know—as no one else in the country works. Fate beats me on without rest; at times I suffer unendurably and I see no light ahead. I have no hope; I do not like people. It is long since I have loved anyone.

SONIA.   You love no one?

ASTROV.   Not a soul. I only feel a sort of tenderness for your old nurse for old times' sake. The peasants are all alike; they are stupid and live in dirt, and the educated people are hard to get along with. One gets tired of them. All our good friends are petty and shallow and see no farther than their own noses; in one word, they are dull. Those that have brains are hysterical, devoured with a mania for self-analysis. They whine, they hate, they pick faults everywhere with unhealthy sharpness. They sneak up to me sideways, look at me out of a corner of the eye, and say: "That man is a lunatic," "That man is a windbag." Or, if they don't know what else to label me with, they say I am strange. I like the woods; that is strange. I don't eat meat; that is strange, too. Simple, natural relations between man and man or man and nature do not exist.

[*He tries to go out*; SONIA *prevents him.*

SONIA.   I beg you, I implore you, not to drink anymore!

ASTROV.   Why not?

SONIA.   It is so unworthy of you. You are well bred, your voice is sweet, you are even—more than anyone I know—handsome. Why do you want to resemble the common people that drink and play cards? Oh, don't, I beg you! You always say that people do not create anything, but only destroy what heaven has given them. Why, oh, why, do you destroy yourself? Oh, don't, I implore you not to! I entreat you!

ASTROV.   [*Gives her his hand*] I won't drink anymore.

SONIA.   Promise me.

ASTROV.   I give you my word of honor.

SONIA.   [*Squeezing his hand*] Thank you.

ASTROV.   I have done with it. You see, I am perfectly sober again, and so I shall stay until the end of my life. [*He looks at his watch*] But, as I was saying, life holds nothing for me; my race is run. I am old, I am tired, I am trivial; my sensibilities are dead. I could never attach myself to anyone again. I love no one, and—never shall! Beauty alone has the power to touch me still. I am deeply moved by it. Helena could turn my head in a day if she wanted to, but that is not love, that is not affection——

[*He shudders and covers his face with his hands.*

SONIA. What is it?

ASTROV. Nothing. During Lent one of my patients died under chloroform.

SONIA. It is time to forget that. [*A pause*] Tell me, doctor, if I had a friend or a younger sister, and if you knew that she, well— loved you, what would you do?

ASTROV. [*Shrugging his shoulders*] I don't know. I don't think I would do anything. I would make her understand that I could not return her love—however, my mind is not bothered about those things now. I must start at once if I am ever to get off. Good-bye, my dear girl. At this rate we shall stand here talking until morning. [*He shakes hands with her*] I shall go out through the sitting room, because I am afraid your uncle might detain me.

[*He goes out.*

SONIA. [*Alone*] Not a word! His heart and soul are still locked from me, and yet for some reason I am strangely happy. I wonder why? [*She laughs with pleasure*] I told him that he was well bred and handsome and that his voice was sweet. Was that a mistake? I can still feel his voice vibrating in the air; it caresses me. [*Wringing her hands*] Oh! How terrible it is to be plain! I am plain, I know it. As I came out of church last Sunday I overheard a woman say, "She is a dear, noble girl, but what a pity she is so ugly!" So ugly!

HELENA *comes in and throws open the window.*

HELENA. The storm is over. What delicious air! [*A pause*] Where is the doctor?

SONIA. He has gone.

[*A pause.*

HELENA. Sonia!

SONIA. Yes?

HELENA. How much longer are you going to sulk at me? We have not hurt each other. Why not be friends? We have had enough of this.

SONIA. I myself— [*She embraces* HELENA] Let us make peace.

HELENA. With all my heart.

[*They are both moved.*

SONIA. Has papa gone to bed?

HELENA. No, he is sitting up in the drawing room. Heaven knows what reason you and I had for not speaking to each other for weeks. [*Sees the open sideboard*] Who left the sideboard open?

SONIA. Dr. Astrov has just had supper.

HELENA. There is some wine. Let us seal our friendship.

SONIA. Yes, let us.

HELENA. Out of one glass. [*She fills a wineglass*] So, we are friends, are we?

SONIA. Yes. [*They drink and kiss each other*] I have long wanted to make friends, but somehow, I was ashamed to.

[*She weeps.*

HELENA. Why are you crying?

SONIA. I don't know. It is nothing.

HELENA. There, there, don't cry. [*She weeps*] Silly! Now I am crying too. [*A pause*] You are angry with me because I seem to have married your father for his money, but don't believe the gossip you hear. I swear to you I married him for love. I was fascinated by his fame and learning. I know now that it was not real love, but it seemed real at the time. I am innocent, and yet your clever, suspicious eyes have been punishing me for an imaginary crime ever since my marriage.

SONIA. Peace, peace! Let us forget the past.

HELENA. You must not look so at people. It is not becoming to you. You must trust people, or life becomes impossible.

SONIA. Tell me truly, as a friend, are you happy?

HELENA. Truly, no.

SONIA. I knew it. One more question: do you wish your husband were young?

HELENA. What a child you are! Of course I do. Go on, ask something else.

SONIA.   Do you like the doctor?

HELENA.   Yes, very much indeed.

SONIA.   [*Laughing*] I have a stupid face, haven't I? He has just gone out, and his voice is still in my ears; I hear his step; I see his face in the dark window. Let me say all I have in my heart! But no, I cannot speak of it so loudly. I am ashamed. Come to my room and let me tell you there. I seem foolish to you, don't I? Talk to me of him.

HELENA.   What can I say?

SONIA.   He is clever. He can do everything. He can cure the sick, and plant woods.

HELENA.   It is not a question of medicine and woods, my dear, he is a man of genius. Do you know what that means? It means he is brave, profound, and of clear insight. He plants a tree and his mind travels a thousand years into the future, and he sees visions of the happiness of the human race. People like him are rare and should be loved. What if he does drink and act roughly at times? A man of genius cannot be a saint in Russia. There he lives, cut off from the world by cold and storm and endless roads of bottomless mud, surrounded by a rough people who are crushed by poverty and disease, his life one continuous struggle, with never a day's respite; how can a man live like that for forty years and keep himself sober and unspotted? [*Kissing* SONIA] I wish you happiness with all my heart; you deserve it. [*She gets up*] As for me, I am a worthless, futile woman. I have always been futile; in music, in love, in my husband's house—in a word, in everything. When you come to think of it, Sonia, I am really very, very unhappy. [*Walks excitedly up and down*] Happiness can never exist for me in this world. Never. Why do you laugh?

SONIA.   [*Laughing and covering her face with her hands*] I am so happy, so happy!

HELENA.   I want to hear music. I might play a little.

SONIA.   Oh, do, do! [*She embraces her*] I could not possibly go to sleep now. Do play!

HELENA.   Yes, I will. Your father is still awake. Music irritates

him when he is ill, but if he says I may, then I shall play a little.
Go, Sonia, and ask him.

SONIA.   Very well.

> [*She goes out. The* WATCHMAN's *rattle is heard in the gar-
> den.*

HELENA.   It is long since I have heard music. And now, I shall
sit and play, and weep like a fool. [*Speaking out of the window*] Is
that you rattling out there, Ephim?

VOICE OF THE WATCHMAN.   It is I.

HELENA.   Don't make such a noise. Your master is ill.

VOICE OF THE WATCHMAN.   I am going away this minute.

> [*Whistles a tune.*

SONIA.   [*Comes back*] He says, no.

> *The curtain falls.*

ACT III

The drawing room of SEREBRAKOV's *house. There are three doors: one to the right, one to the left, and one in the center of the room.* VOITSKI *and* SONIA *are sitting down.* HELENA *is walking up and down, absorbed in thought.*

VOITSKI.   We were asked by the professor to be here at one o'clock. [*Looks at his watch*] It is now a quarter to one. It seems he has some communication to make to the world.

HELENA.   Probably a matter of business.

VOITSKI.   He never had any business. He writes twaddle, grumbles, and eats his heart out with jealousy; that's all he does.

SONIA.   [*Reproachfully*] Uncle!

VOITSKI.   All right. I beg your pardon. [*He points to* HELENA] Look at her. Wandering up and down from sheer idleness. A sweet picture, really.

HELENA.   I wonder you are not bored, droning on in the same key from morning until night. [*Despairingly*] I am dying of this tedium. What shall I do?

SONIA.   [*Shrugging her shoulders*] There is plenty to do if you would.

HELENA.   For instance?

SONIA.   You could help run this place, teach the children, care for the sick—isn't that enough? Before you and Papa came, Uncle Vanya and I used to go to market ourselves to deal in flour.

HELENA.   I don't know anything about such things, and be-

28

sides, they don't interest me. It is only in novels that women go out and teach and heal the peasants; how can I suddenly begin to do it?

SONIA.   How can you live here and not do it? Wait awhile, you will get used to it all. [*Embraces her*] Don't be sad, dearest. [*Laughing*] You feel miserable and restless, and can't seem to fit into this life, and your restlessness is catching. Look at Uncle Vanya, he does nothing now but haunt you like a shadow, and I have left my work today to come here and talk with you. I am getting lazy, and don't want to go on with it. Dr. Astrov hardly ever used to come here; it was all we could do to persuade him to visit us once a month, and now he has abandoned his forestry and his practice, and comes every day. You must be a witch.

VOITSKI.   Why should you languish here? Come, my dearest, my beauty, be sensible! The blood of a nixie runs in your veins. Oh, won't you let yourself be one? Give your nature the reins for once in your life; fall head over ears in love with some other water sprite and plunge down head first into a deep pool, so that the Herr Professor and all of us may have our hands free again.

HELENA.   [*Angrily*] Leave me alone! How cruel you are!

[*She tries to go out.*

VOITSKI.   [*Preventing her*] There, there, my beauty, I apologize. [*He kisses her hand*] Forgive me.

HELENA.   Confess that you would try the patience of an angel.

VOITSKI.   As a peace offering I am going to fetch some flowers that I picked for you this morning: some autumn roses, beautiful, sorrowful roses.

[*He goes out.*

SONIA.   Autumn roses, beautiful, sorrowful roses!

[*She and* HELENA *stand looking out of the window.*

HELENA.   September already! How shall we live through the long winter here? [*A pause*] Where is the doctor?

SONIA.   He is writing in Uncle Vanya's room. I am glad Uncle Vanya has gone out, I want to talk to you about something.

HELENA.   About what?

SONIA.   About what?

> [*She lays her head on* HELENA's *breast.*

HELENA.   [*Stroking her hair*] There, there, that will do. Don't, Sonia.

SONIA.   I am ugly!

HELENA.   You have lovely hair.

SONIA.   Don't say that! [*She turns to look at herself in the glass*] No, when a woman is ugly they always say she has beautiful hair or eyes. I have loved him now for six years; I have loved him more than one loves one's mother. I seem to hear him beside me every moment of the day. I feel the pressure of his hand on mine. If I look up, I seem to see him coming, and as you see, I run to you to talk of him. He is here every day now, but he never looks at me, he does not notice my presence. It is agony. I have absolutely no hope, no, no hope. Oh, my God! Give me strength to endure. I prayed all last night. I often go up to him and speak to him and look into his eyes. My pride is gone. I am not mistress of myself. Yesterday I told Uncle Vanya. I couldn't control myself, and all the servants know it. Everyone knows that I love him.

HELENA.   Does he?

SONIA.   No, he never notices me.

HELENA.   [*Thoughtfully*] He is a strange man. Listen, Sonia, will you allow me to speak to him? I shall be careful, only hint. [*A pause*] Really, to be in uncertainty all these years! Let me do it!

> SONIA *nods an affirmative.*

HELENA.   Splendid! It will be easy to find out whether he loves you or not. Don't be ashamed, sweetheart, don't worry. I shall be careful; he will not notice a thing. We only want to find out whether it is yes or no, don't we? [*A pause*] And if it is no, then he must keep away from here, is that so?

> SONIA *nods.*

HELENA.   It will be easier not to see him anymore. We won't put off the examination an instant. He said he had a sketch to show me. Go and tell him at once that I want to see him.

SONIA.   [*In great excitement*] Will you tell me the whole truth?

HELENA.   Of course I will. I am sure that no matter what it is, it will be easier for you to bear than this uncertainty. Trust me, dearest.

SONIA.   Yes, yes. I shall say that you want to see his sketch. [*She starts out, but stops near the door and looks back*] No, it is better not to know—and yet—there may be hope.

HELENA.   What do you say?

SONIA.   Nothing.

[*She goes out.*

HELENA.   [*Alone*] There is no greater sorrow than to know another's secret when you cannot help them. [*In deep thought*] He is obviously not in love with her, but why shouldn't he marry her? She is not pretty, but she is so clever and pure and good, she would make a splendid wife for a country doctor of his years. [*A pause*] I can understand how the poor child feels. She lives here in this desperate loneliness with no one around her except these colorless shadows that go mooning about talking nonsense and knowing nothing except that they eat, drink, and sleep. Among them appears from time to time this Dr. Astrov, so different, so handsome, so interesting, so charming. It is like seeing the moon rise on a dark night. Oh, to surrender oneself to his embrace! To lose oneself in his arms! I am a little in love with him myself! Yes, I am lonely without him, and when I think of him I smile. That Uncle Vanya says I have the blood of a nixie in my veins: "Give rein to your nature for once in your life!" Perhaps it is right that I should. Oh, to be free as a bird, to fly away from all your sleepy faces and your talk and forget that you have existed at all! But I am a coward, I am afraid; my conscience torments me. He comes here every day now. I can guess why, and feel guilty already; I should like to fall on my knees at Sonia's feet and beg her forgiveness, and weep.

ASTROV *comes in carrying a portfolio.*

ASTROV.   How do you do? [*Shakes hands with her*] Do you want to see my sketch?
HELENA.   Yes, you promised to show me what you had been doing. Have you time now?
ASTROV.   Of course I have!

He lays the portfolio on the table, takes out the sketch and fastens it to the table with thumbtacks.

ASTROV.   Where were you born?
HELENA.   [*Helping him*] In St. Petersburg.
ASTROV.   And educated?
HELENA.   At the Conservatory there.
ASTROV.   You don't find this life very interesting, I dare say?
HELENA.   Oh, why not? It is true I don't know the country very well, but I have read a great deal about it.
ASTROV.   I have my own desk there in Ivan's room. When I am absolutely too exhausted to go on I drop everything and rush over here to forget myself in this work for an hour or two. Ivan and Miss Sonia sit rattling at their counting boards, the cricket chirps, and I sit beside them and paint, feeling warm and peaceful. But I don't permit myself this luxury very often, only once a month. [*Pointing to the picture*] Look there! That is a map of our region as it was fifty years ago. The green tints, both dark and light, represent forests. Half the map, as you see, is covered with it. Where the green is striped with red the forests were inhabited by elk and wild goats. Here, on this lake, lived great flocks of swans and geese and ducks; as the old folks say, there was a power of birds of every kind. Now they have vanished like a cloud. Beside the hamlets and villages, you see, I have dotted down here and there the various settlements, farms, hermit's caves, and water mills. This district carried a great many cattle and horses, as you can see by the quantity of blue paint. For instance, see how thickly it lies in this part; there were great herds of them here, an average of three horses to every house. [*A pause*] Now, look lower down. This is the region as it was

twenty-five years ago. Only a third of the map is green now with forests. There are no goats left and no elk. The blue paint is lighter, and so on, and so on. Now we come to the third part; our region as it appears today. We still see spots of green, but not much. The elk, the swans, the blackcock have disappeared. It is, on the whole, the picture of a regular and slow decline which it will evidently only take about ten or fifteen more years to complete. You may perhaps object that it is the march of progress, that the old order must give place to the new, and you might be right if roads had been run through these ruined woods, or if factories and schools had taken their place. The people then would have become better educated and healthier and richer, but as it is, we have nothing of the sort. We have the same swamps and mosquitoes; the same disease and want; the typhoid, the diphtheria, the burning villages. We are confronted by the degradation of our country, brought on by the fierce struggle for existence of the human race. It is the consequence of the ignorance and unconsciousness of starving, shivering, sick humanity that, to save its children, instinctively snatches at everything that can warm it and still its hunger. So it destroys everything it can lay its hands on, without a thought for the morrow. And almost everything has gone, and nothing has been created to take its place. [*Coldly*] But I see by your face that I am not interesting you.

HELENA. I know so little about such things!

ASTROV. There is nothing to know. It simply isn't interesting, that's all.

HELENA. Frankly, my thoughts were elsewhere. Forgive me! I want to submit you to a little examination, but I am embarrassed and don't know how to begin.

ASTROV. An examination?

HELENA. Yes, but quite an innocent one. Sit down. [*They sit down*] It is about a certain young girl I know. Let us discuss it like honest people, like friends, and then forget what has passed between us, shall we?

ASTROV. Very well.

HELENA.   It is about my stepdaughter, Sonia. Do you like her?

ASTROV.   Yes, I respect her.

HELENA.   Do you like her—as a woman?

ASTROV.   [*Slowly*] No.

HELENA.   One more word, and that will be the last. You have not noticed anything?

ASTROV.   No, nothing.

HELENA.   [*Taking his hand*] You do not love her. I see that in your eyes. She is suffering. You must realize that, and not come here anymore.

ASTROV.   My sun has set, yes, and then I haven't the time. [*Shrugging his shoulders*] Where shall I find time for such things?

[*He is embarrassed.*

HELENA.   Bah! What an unpleasant conversation! I am as out of breath as if I had been running three miles uphill. Thank heaven, that is over! Now let us forget everything as if nothing had been said. You are sensible. You understand. [*A pause*] I am actually blushing.

ASTROV.   If you had spoken a month ago I might perhaps have considered it, but now— [*He shrugs his shoulders*] Of course, if she is suffering—but I cannot understand why you had to put me through this examination. [*He searches her face with his eyes, and shakes his finger at her*] Oho, you are wily!

HELENA.   What does this mean?

ASTROV.   [*Laughing*] You are a wily one! I admit that Sonia is suffering, but what does this examination of yours mean? [*He prevents her from retorting, and goes on quickly*] Please don't put on such a look of surprise; you know perfectly well why I come here every day. Yes, you know perfectly why and for whose sake I come! Oh, my sweet tigress! Don't look at me in that way; I am an old bird!

HELENA.   [*Perplexed*] A tigress? I don't understand you.

ASTROV.   Beautiful, sleek tigress, you must have your victims! For a whole month I have done nothing but seek you eagerly. I have thrown over everything for you, and you love to see it. Now then, I am sure you knew all this without putting me through your examination. [*Crossing his arms and bowing his head*] I surrender. Here you have me—now, eat me.

HELENA.   You have gone mad!

ASTROV.   You are afraid!

HELENA.   I am a better and stronger woman than you think me. Good-bye.

[*She tries to leave the room.*

ASTROV.   Why good-bye? Don't say good-bye, don't waste words. Oh, how lovely you are—what hands!

[*He kisses her hands.*

HELENA.   Enough of this! [*She frees her hands*] Leave the room! You have forgotten yourself.

ASTROV.   Tell me, tell me, where can we meet tomorrow? [*He puts his arm around her*] Don't you see that we must meet, that it is inevitable?

He kisses her. VOITSKI *comes in carrying a bunch of roses, and stops in the doorway.*

HELENA.   [*Without seeing* VOITSKI] Have pity! Leave me! [*Lays her head on* ASTROV's *shoulder*] Don't!

[*She tries to break away from him.*

ASTROV.   [*Holding her by the waist*] Be in the forest tomorrow at two o'clock. Will you? Will you?

HELENA.   [*Sees* VOITSKI] Let me go! [*Goes to the window, deeply embarrassed*] This is appalling!

VOITSKI.   [*Throws the flowers on a chair, and speaks in great excitement, wiping his face with his handkerchief*] Nothing—yes, yes, nothing.

ASTROV.   The weather is fine today, my dear Ivan; the morning was overcast and looked like rain, but now the sun is shining again. Honestly, we have had a very fine autumn, and the wheat is looking fairly well. [*Puts his map back into the portfolio*] But the days are growing short.

[*He goes out.*

HELENA. [*Goes quickly up to* VOITSKI] You must do your best; you must use all your power to get my husband and myself away from here today! Do you hear? I say, this very day!

VOITSKI. [*Wiping his face*] Oh! Ah! Oh! All right! I— Helena, I saw everything!

HELENA. [*In great agitation*] Do you hear me? I must leave here this very day.

SEREBRAKOV, SONIA, MARINA, *and* TELEGIN *come in.*

TELEGIN. I am not very well myself, your Excellency. I have been limping for two days, and my head——

SEREBRAKOV. Where are the others? I hate this house. It is a regular labyrinth. Everyone is always scattered through the twenty-six enormous rooms; one never can find a soul. [*Rings*] Ask my wife and Madame Voitskaya to come here!

HELENA. I am here already.

SEREBRAKOV. Please, all of you, sit down.

SONIA. [*Goes up to* HELENA *and asks anxiously*] What did he say?

HELENA. I'll tell you later.

SONIA. You are moved. [*Looking quickly and inquiringly into her face*] I understand; he said he would not come here anymore. [*A pause*] Tell me, did he?

HELENA *nods.*

SEREBRAKOV. [*To* TELEGIN] One can, after all, become reconciled to being an invalid, but not to this country life. The ways of it stick in my throat and I feel exactly as if I had been whirled off the earth and landed on a strange planet. Please be seated, ladies and gentlemen. Sonia! [SONIA *does not hear. She is standing with her head bowed sadly forward on her breast*] Sonia! [*A pause*] She does not hear me. [*To* MARINA] Sit down too, nurse. [MARINA *sits down and begins to knit her stocking*] I crave your indulgence, ladies and gentlemen; hang your ears, if I may say so, on the peg of attention.

[*He laughs.*

VOITSKI.   [*Agitated*] Perhaps you do not need me—may I be excused?

SEREBRAKOV.   No, you are needed now more than anyone.

VOITSKI.   What is it you want of me?

SEREBRAKOV.   You—but what are you angry about? If it is anything I have done, I ask you to forgive me.

VOITSKI.   Oh, drop that and come to business; what do you want?

MME. VOITSKAYA *comes in.*

SEREBRAKOV.   Here is Mother. Ladies and gentlemen, I shall begin. I have asked you to assemble here, my friends, in order to discuss a very important matter. I want to ask you for your assistance and advice, and knowing your unfailing amiability I think I can count on both. I am a bookworm and a scholar, and am unfamiliar with practical affairs. I cannot, I find, dispense with the help of well-informed people such as you, Ivan, and you, Telegin, and you, Mother. The truth is, *manet omnes una nox*, that is to say, our lives are in the hands of God, and as I am old and ill, I realize that the time has come for me to dispose of my property in regard to the interests of my family. My life is nearly over, and I am not thinking of myself, but I have a young wife and daughter. [*A pause*] I cannot continue to live in the country; we were not made for country life, and yet we cannot afford to live in town on the income derived from this estate. We might sell the woods, but that would be an expedient we could not resort to every year. We must find some means of guaranteeing to ourselves a certain more or less fixed yearly income. With this object in view, a plan has occurred to me which I now have the honor of presenting to you for your consideration. I shall only give you a rough outline, avoiding all details. Our estate does not pay on an average more than two percent on the money invested in it. I propose to sell it. If we then invest our capital in bonds, it will earn us four to five percent, and we should probably have a surplus over of several thousand rubles, with which we could buy a summer cottage in Finland——

VOITSKI. Hold on! Repeat what you just said; I don't think I heard you quite right.

SEREBRAKOV. I said we would invest the money in bonds and buy a cottage in Finland with the surplus.

VOITSKI. No, not Finland—you said something else.

SEREBRAKOV. I propose to sell this place.

VOITSKI. Aha! That was it! So you are going to sell the place? Splendid. The idea is a rich one. And what do you propose to do with my old mother and me and with Sonia here?

SEREBRAKOV. That will be decided in due time. We can't do everything at once.

VOITSKI. Wait! It is clear that until this moment I have never had a grain of sense in my head. I have always been stupid enough to think that the estate belonged to Sonia. My father bought it as a wedding present for my sister, and I foolishly imagined that as our laws were made for Russians and not Turks, my sister's estate would come down to her child.

SEREBRAKOV. Of course it is Sonia's. Has anyone denied it? I don't want to sell it without Sonia's consent; on the contrary, what I am doing is for Sonia's good.

VOITSKI. This is absolutely incomprehensible. Either I have gone mad or—or——

MME. VOITSKAYA. Jean, don't contradict Alexander. Trust him; he knows better than we do what is right and what is wrong.

VOITSKI. I shan't. Give me some water. [*He drinks*] Go ahead! Say anything you please—anything!

SEREBRAKOV. I can't imagine why you are so upset. I don't pretend that my scheme is an ideal one, and if you all object to it I shall not insist.

[*A pause.*

TELEGIN. [*With embarrassment*] I not only nourish feelings of respect toward learning, your Excellency, but I am also drawn to it by family ties. My brother Gregory's wife's brother, whom you may know; his name is Constantine Lakedemonov, and he used to be a magistrate—

VOITSKI. Stop, Waffles. This is business; wait a bit, we will talk of that later. [*To* SEREBRAKOV] There now, ask him what he thinks; this estate was bought from his uncle.

SEREBRAKOV.   Ah! Why should I ask questions? What good would it do?

VOITSKI.   The price was ninety-five thousand rubles. My father paid seventy and left a debt of twenty-five. Now listen! This place could never have been bought had I not renounced my inheritance in favor of my sister, whom I deeply loved—and what is more, I worked for ten years like an ox, and paid off the debt.

SEREBRAKOV.   I regret ever having started this conversation.

VOITSKI.   Thanks entirely to my own personal efforts, the place is entirely clear of debts, and now, when I have grown old, you want to throw me out, neck and crop!

SEREBRAKOV.   I can't imagine what you are driving at.

VOITSKI.   For twenty-five years I have managed this place, and have sent you the returns from it like the most honest of servants, and you have never given me one single word of thanks for my work, not one—neither in my youth nor now. You allowed me a meager salary of five hundred rubles a year, a beggar's pittance, and have never even thought of adding a ruble to it.

SEREBRAKOV.   What did I know about such things, Ivan? I am not a practical man and don't understand them. You might have helped yourself to all you wanted.

VOITSKI.   Yes, why did I not steal? Don't you all despise me for not stealing, when it would have been only justice? And I should not now have been a beggar!

MME. VOITSKAYA.   [*Sternly*] Jean!

TELEGIN.   [*Agitated*] Vanya, old man, don't talk in that way. Why spoil such pleasant relations? [*He embraces him*] Do stop!

VOITSKI.   For twenty-five years I have been sitting here with my mother like a mole in a burrow. Our every thought and hope was yours and yours only. By day we talked with pride of you and your work, and spoke your name with veneration; our nights we wasted reading the books and papers which my soul now loathes.

TELEGIN.   Don't, Vanya, don't. I can't stand it.

SEREBRAKOV.   [*Wrathfully*] What under heaven do you want,
anyway?

VOITSKI.   We used to think of you as almost superhuman, but
now the scales have fallen from my eyes and I see you as you are!
You write on art without knowing anything about it. Those books
of yours, which I used to admire, are not worth one copper
kopeck. You are a hoax!

SEREBRAKOV.   Can't anyone make him stop? I am going!

HELENA.   Ivan, I command you to stop this instant! Do you
hear me?

VOITSKI.   I refuse! [SEREBRAKOV *tries to get out of the room,
but* VOITSKI *bars the door*] Wait! I have not done yet! You have
wrecked my life. I have never lived. My best years have gone for
nothing, have been ruined, thanks to you. You are my most bitter enemy!

TELEGIN.   I can't stand it; I can't stand it. I am going.

[*He goes out in great excitement.*

SEREBRAKOV.   But what do you want? What earthly right have
you to use such language to me? Ruination! If this estate is yours,
then take it, and let me be ruined!

HELENA.   I am going away out of this hell this minute.
[*Shrieks*] This is too much!

VOITSKI.   My life has been a failure. I am clever and brave
and strong. If I had lived a normal life I might have become another Schopenhauer or Dostoevski. I am losing my head! I am
going crazy! Mother, I am in despair! Oh, Mother!

MME. VOITSKAYA.   [*Sternly*] Listen, Alexander!

SONIA *falls on her knees beside the nurse and nestles against
her.*

SONIA.   Oh, nurse, nurse!

VOITSKI.   Mother! What shall I do? But no, don't speak! I
know what to do. [*To* SEREBRAKOV] And you will understand me!

*He goes out through the door in the center of the room and
MME. VOITSKAYA follows him.*

SEREBRAKOV.   Tell me, what on earth is the matter? Take this lunatic out of my sight! I cannot possibly live under the same roof with him. His room [*He points to the center door*] is almost next door to mine. Let him take himself off into the village or into the wing of the house, or I shall leave here at once. I cannot stay in the same house with him.

HELENA.   [*To her husband*] We are leaving today; we must get ready at once for our departure.

SEREBRAKOV.   What a perfectly dreadful man!

SONIA.   [*On her knees beside the nurse and turning to her father. She speaks with emotion*] You must be kind to us, Papa. Uncle Vanya and I are so unhappy! [*Controlling her despair*] Have pity on us. Remember how Uncle Vanya and Granny used to copy and translate your books for you every night—every, every night. Uncle Vanya has toiled without rest; he would never spend a penny on us, we sent it all to you. We have not eaten the bread of idleness. I am not saying this as I would like to, but you must understand us, Papa, you must be merciful to us.

HELENA.   [*Very excited, to her husband*] For heaven's sake, Alexander, go and have a talk with him—explain!

SEREBRAKOV.   Very well, I shall have a talk with him, but I won't apologize for a thing. I am not angry with him, but you must confess that his behavior has been strange, to say the least. Excuse me, I shall go to him.

　　　　　　　　　　　　　[*He goes out through the center door.*

HELENA.   Be gentle with him; try to quiet him.

　　　　　　　　　　　　　　　　　[*She follows him out.*

SONIA.   [*Nestling nearer to* MARINA] Nurse, oh, nurse!

MARINA.   It's all right, my baby. When the geese have cackled they will be still again. First they cackle and then they stop.

SONIA.   Nurse!

MARINA.   You are trembling all over, as if you were freezing. There, there, little orphan baby, God is merciful. A little linden tea, and it will all pass away. Don't cry, my sweetest. [*Looking angrily at the door in the center of the room*] See, the geese have all gone now. The devil take them!

A *shot is heard.* HELENA *screams behind the scenes.* SONIA *shudders.*

MARINA.   Bang! What's that?

SEREBRAKOV.   [*Comes in reeling with terror*] Hold him! Hold him! He has gone mad!

HELENA *and* VOITSKI *are seen struggling in the doorway.*

HELENA.   [*Trying to wrest the revolver from him*] Give it to me; give it to me, I tell you!

VOITSKI.   Let me go, Helena, let me go! [*He frees himself and rushes in, looking everywhere for* SEREBRAKOV] Where is he? Ah, there he is! [*He shoots at him. A pause*] I didn't get him? I missed again? [*Furiously*] Damnation! Damnation! To hell with him!

He *flings the revolver on the floor, and drops helpless into a chair.* SEREBRAKOV *stands as if stupefied.* HELENA *leans against the wall, almost fainting.*

HELENA.   Take me away! Take me away! I can't stay here—I can't!

VOITSKI.   [*In despair*] Oh, what shall I do? What shall I do?

SONIA.   [*Softly*] Oh, nurse, nurse!

The curtain falls.

ACT IV

VOITSKI's *bedroom, which is also his office. A table stands near the window; on it are ledgers, letter scales, and papers of every description. Nearby stands a smaller table belonging to* ASTROV, *with his paints and drawing materials. On the wall hangs a cage containing a starling. There is also a map of Africa on the wall, obviously of no use to anybody. There is a large sofa covered with buckram. A door to the left leads into an inner room; one to the right leads into the front hall, and before this door lies a mat for the peasants with their muddy boots to stand on. It is an autumn evening. The silence is profound.* TELEGIN *and* MARINA *are sitting facing one another, winding wool.*

TELEGIN.   Be quick, Marina, or we shall be called away to say good-bye before you have finished. The carriage has already been ordered.

MARINA.   [*Trying to wind more quickly*] I am a little tired.

TELEGIN.   They are going to Kharkov to live.

MARINA.   They do well to go.

TELEGIN.   They have been frightened. The professor's wife won't stay here an hour longer. "If we are going at all, let's be off," says she, "we shall go to Kharkov and look about us, and then we can send for our things." They are traveling light. It seems, Marina, that fate has decreed for them not to live here.

MARINA.   And quite rightly. What a storm they have just raised! It was shameful!

43

TELEGIN.   It was indeed. The scene was worthy of the brush of Aibazofski.

MARINA.   I wish I'd never laid eyes on them. [*A pause*] Now we shall have things as they were again: tea at eight, dinner at one, and supper in the evening; everything in order as decent folks, as Christians like to have it. [*Sighs*] It is a long time since I have eaten noodles.

TELEGIN.   Yes, we haven't had noodles for ages. [*A pause*] Not for ages. As I was going through the village this morning, Marina, one of the shopkeepers called after me, "Hi, you hanger-on!" I felt it bitterly.

MARINA.   Don't pay the least attention to them, master; we are all dependents on God. You and Sonia and all of us. Everyone must work, no one can sit idle. Where is Sonia?

TELEGIN.   In the garden with the doctor, looking for Ivan. They fear he may lay violent hands on himself.

MARINA.   Where is his pistol?

TELEGIN.   [*Whispers*] I hid it in the cellar.

VOITSKI *and* ASTROV *come in.*

VOITSKI.   Leave me alone! [*To* MARINA *and* TELEGIN] Go away! Go away and leave me to myself, if but for an hour. I won't have you watching me like this!

TELEGIN.   Yes, yes, Vanya.

[*He goes out on tiptoe.*

MARINA.   The gander cackles; ho! ho! ho!

[*She gathers up her wool and goes out.*

VOITSKI.   Leave me by myself!

ASTROV.   I would, with the greatest pleasure. I ought to have gone long ago, but I shan't leave you until you have returned what you took from me.

VOITSKI.   I took nothing from you.

ASTROV.   I am not jesting, don't detain me, I really must go.

VOITSKI.   I took nothing of yours.

ASTROV.   You didn't? Very well, I shall have to wait a little longer, and then you will have to forgive me if I resort to force. We shall have to bind you and search you. I mean what I say.

VOITSKI.   Do as you please. [*A pause*] Oh, to make such a fool of myself! To shoot twice and miss him both times! I shall never forgive myself.

ASTROV.   When the impulse came to shoot, it would have been as well had you put a bullet through your own head.

VOITSKI.   [*Shrugging his shoulders*] Strange! I attempted murder, and am not going to be arrested or brought to trial. That means they think me mad. [*With a bitter laugh*] Me! I am mad, and those who hide their worthlessness, their dullness, their crying heartlessness behind a professor's mask, are sane! Those who marry old men and then deceive them under the noses of all, are sane! I saw you kiss her; I saw you in each other's arms!

ASTROV.   Yes, sir, I did kiss her; so there.

[*He puts his thumb to his nose.*

VOITSKI.   [*His eyes on the door*] No, it is the earth that is mad, because she still bears us on her breast.

ASTROV.   That is nonsense.

VOITSKI.   Well? Am I not a madman, and therefore irresponsible? Haven't I the right to talk nonsense?

ASTROV.   This is a farce! You are not mad; you are simply a ridiculous fool. I used to think every fool was out of his senses, but now I see that lack of sense is a man's normal state, and you are perfectly normal.

VOITSKI.   [*Covers his face with his hands*] Oh! If you knew how ashamed I am! These piercing pangs of shame are like nothing on earth. [*In an agonized voice*] I can't endure them! [*He leans against the table*] What can I do? What can I do?

ASTROV.   Nothing.

VOITSKI.   You must tell me something! Oh, my God! I am forty-seven years old. I may live to sixty; I still have thirteen years before me; an eternity! How shall I be able to endure life for thirteen years? What shall I do? How can I fill them? Oh, don't you see? [*He presses* ASTROV's *hand convulsively*] Don't you see, if only I could live the rest of my life in some new way! If I could only wake some still, bright morning and feel that life had begun again; that the past was forgotten and had vanished like smoke. [*He weeps*] Oh, to begin life anew! Tell me, tell me how to begin.

ASTROV. [*Crossly*] What nonsense! What sort of a new life can you and I look forward to? We can have no hope.

VOITSKI. None?

ASTROV. None. Of that I am convinced.

VOITSKI. Tell me what to do. [*He puts his hand to his heart*] I feel such a burning pain here.

ASTROV. [*Shouts angrily*] Stop! [*Then, more gently*] It may be that posterity, which will despise us for our blind and stupid lives, will find some road to happiness; but we—you and I—have but one hope, the hope that we may be visited by visions, perhaps by pleasant ones, as we lie resting in our graves. [*Sighing*] Yes, brother, there were only two respectable, intelligent men in this district, you and I. Ten years or so of this life of ours, this miserable life, have sucked us under, and we have become as contemptible and petty as the rest. But don't try to talk me out of my purpose! Give me what you took from me, will you?

VOITSKI. I took nothing from you.

ASTROV. You took a little bottle of morphine out of my medicine case. [*A pause*] Listen! If you are positively determined to make an end to yourself, go into the woods and shoot yourself there. Give up the morphine, or there will be a lot of talk and guesswork; people will think I gave it to you. I don't fancy having to perform a postmortem on you. Do you think I would find it interesting?

SONIA *comes in.*

VOITSKI. Leave me alone.

ASTROV. [*To* SONIA] Sonia, your uncle has stolen a bottle of morphine out of my medicine case and won't give it up. Tell him that his behavior is—well, unwise. I haven't time, I must be going.

SONIA. Uncle Vanya, did you take the morphine?

ASTROV. Yes, he took it. [*A pause*] I am absolutely sure.

SONIA. Give it up! Why do you want to frighten us? [*Tenderly*] Give it up, Uncle Vanya! My misfortune is perhaps even greater than yours, but I am not plunged in despair. I endure my sorrow, and shall endure it until my life comes to a natural end. You must endure yours, too. [*A pause*] Give it up! Dear, darling Uncle Vanya. Give it up! [*She weeps*] You are so good, I am sure you will have pity on us and give it up. You must endure your sorrow, Uncle Vanya; you must endure it.

VOITSKI *takes a bottle from the drawer of the table and hands it to* ASTROV.

VOITSKI. There it is! [*To* SONIA] And now, we must get to work at once; we must do something, or else I shall not be able to endure it.

SONIA. Yes, yes, to work! As soon as we have seen them off we shall go to work. [*She nervously straightens out the papers on the table*] Everything is in a muddle!

ASTROV. [*Putting the bottle in his case, which he straps together*] Now I can be off.

HELENA *comes in.*

HELENA. Are you here, Ivan? We are starting in a moment. Go to Alexander, he wants to speak to you.

SONIA. Go, Uncle Vanya. [*She takes* VOITSKI'S *arm*] Come, you and Papa must make peace; that is absolutely necessary.

SONIA *and* VOITSKI *go out.*

HELENA. I am going away. [*She gives* ASTROV *her hand*] Good-bye.

ASTROV. So soon?

HELENA. The carriage is waiting.

ASTROV. Good-bye.

HELENA. You promised me you would go away yourself today.

ASTROV. I have not forgotten. I am going at once. [*A pause*] Were you frightened? Was it so terrible?

HELENA.   Yes.

ASTROV.   Couldn't you stay? Couldn't you? Tomorrow—in the forest——

HELENA.   No. It is all settled, and that is why I can look you so bravely in the face. Our departure is fixed. One thing I must ask of you: don't think too badly of me; I would like you to respect me.

ASTROV.   Ah! [*With an impatient gesture*] Stay, I implore you! Confess that there is nothing for you to do in this world. You have no object in life; there is nothing to occupy your attention, and sooner or later your feelings must master you. It is inevitable. It would be better if it happened not in Kharkov or in Kursk, but here, in nature's lap. It would then at least be poetical, even beautiful. Here you have the forests, the houses half in ruins that Turgenev writes of.

HELENA.   How comical you are! I am angry with you and yet I shall always remember you with pleasure. You are interesting and original. You and I will never meet again, and so I shall tell you—why should I conceal it?—that I am just a little in love with you. Come, one more last pressure of our hands, and then let us part good friends. Let us not bear each other any ill will.

ASTROV.   [*Pressing her hand*] Yes, go. [*Thoughtfully*] You seem to be sincere and good, and yet there is something strangely disquieting about all your personality. No sooner did you arrive here with your husband than everyone whom you found busy and actively creating something was forced to drop his work and give himself up for the whole summer to your husband's gout and yourself. You and he have infected us with your idleness. I have been swept off my feet; I have not put my hand to a thing for weeks, during which sickness has been running its course unchecked among the people, and the peasants have been pasturing their cattle in my woods and young plantations. Go where you will, you and your husband will always carry destruction in your train. I am joking, of course, and yet I am strangely sure that had you stayed here we would have been overtaken by the most immense desolation. I would have gone to my ruin, and you—you would not have prospered. So go! *E finita la comedia!*

HELENA.   [*Snatching a pencil off* ASTROV's *table, and hiding it with a quick movement*] I shall take this pencil for memory!

ASTROV.   How strange it is. We meet, and then suddenly it seems that we must part forever. That is the way in this world. As long as we are alone, before Uncle Vanya comes in with a bouquet—allow me—to kiss you good-bye—may I? [*He kisses her on the cheek*] So! Splendid!

HELENA.   I wish you every happiness. [*She glances about her*] For once in my life, I shall, and scorn the consequences! [*She kisses him impetuously, and they quickly part*] I must go.

ASTROV.   Yes, go. If the carriage is there, then start at once.

[*They stand listening.*

ASTROV.   *E finita!*

VOITSKI, SEREBRAKOV, MME. VOITSKAYA *with her book,* TELEGIN, *and* SONIA *come in.*

SEREBRAKOV.   [*To* VOITSKI] Shame on him who bears malice for the past. I have gone through so much in the last few hours that I feel capable of writing a whole treatise on the conduct of life for the instruction of posterity. I gladly accept your apology, and myself ask your forgiveness.

[*He kisses* VOITSKI *three times.*

HELENA *embraces* SONIA.

SEREBRAKOV.   [*Kissing* MME. VOITSKAYA's *hand*] Mother!

MME. VOITSKAYA.   [*Kissing him*] Have your picture taken, Alexander, and send me one. You know how dear you are to me.

TELEGIN.   Good-bye, your Excellency. Don't forget us.

SEREBRAKOV.   [*Kissing his daughter*] Good-bye, good-bye all. [*Shaking hands with* ASTROV] Many thanks for your pleasant company. I have a deep regard for your opinions and your enthusiasm, but let me, as an old man, give one word of advice at parting: do something, my friend! Work! Do something! [*They all bow*] Good luck to you all.

[*He goes out followed by* MME. VOITSKAYA *and* SONIA.
VOITSKI. [*Kissing* HELENA's *hand fervently*] Good-bye—
forgive me! I shall never see you again!
HELENA. [*Touched*] Good-bye, dear boy.

> *She lightly kisses his head as he bends over her hand, and goes out.*

ASTROV. Tell them to bring my carriage around too, Waffles.
TELEGIN. All right, old man.

> ASTROV *and* VOITSKI *are left behind alone.* ASTROV *collects his paints and drawing materials on the table and packs them away in a box.*

ASTROV. Why don't you go to see them off?
VOITSKI. Let them go! I—I can't go out there. I feel too sad. I must go to work on something at once. To work! To work!

> *He rummages through his papers on the table. A pause. The tinkling of bells is heard as the horses trot away.*

ASTROV. They have gone! The professor, I suppose, is glad to go. He couldn't be tempted back now by a fortune.

> MARINA *comes in.*

MARINA. They have gone.
> [*She sits down in an armchair and knits her stocking.*

> SONIA *comes in wiping her eyes.*

SONIA. They have gone. God be with them. [*To her uncle*] And now, Uncle Vanya, let us do something!
VOITSKI. To work! To work!
SONIA. It is long, long, since you and I have sat together at this table. [*She lights a lamp on the table*] No ink! [*She takes the inkstand to the cupboard and fills it from an ink bottle*] How sad it is to see them go!

> MME. VOITSKAYA *comes in slowly.*

MME. VOITSKAYA.   They have gone.

> *She sits down and at once becomes absorbed in her book.*
> SONIA *sits down at the table and looks through an account book.*

SONIA.   First, Uncle Vanya, let us write up the accounts. They are in a dreadful state. Come, begin. You take one and I will take the other.

VOITSKI.   In account with——

> [*They sit silently writing.*

MARINA.   [*Yawning*] The sandman has come.

ASTROV.   How still it is. Their pens scratch, the cricket sings; it is so warm and comfortable. I hate to go.

> [*The tinkling of bells is heard.*

ASTROV.   My carriage has come. There now remains but to say good-bye to you, my friends, and to my table here, and then—away!

> [*He puts the map into the portfolio.*

MARINA.   Don't hurry away; sit a little longer with us.

ASTROV.   Impossible.

VOITSKI.   [*Writing*] And carry forward from the old debt two seventy-five——

> WORKMAN *comes in.*

WORKMAN.   Your carriage is waiting, sir.

ASTROV.   All right. [*He hands* WORKMAN *his medicine case, portfolio, and box*] Look out, don't crush the portfolio!

WORKMAN.   Very well, sir.

SONIA.   When shall we see you again?

ASTROV.   Hardly before next summer. Probably not this winter, though, of course, if anything should happen you will let me know. [*He shakes hands with them*] Thank you for your kindness, for your hospitality, for everything! [*He goes up to* MARINA *and kisses her head*] Good-bye, old nurse!

MARINA.   Are you going without your tea?

ASTROV.   I don't want any, nurse.

MARINA.   Won't you have a drop of vodka?
ASTROV.   [*Hesitatingly*] Yes, I might.

MARINA *goes out.*

ASTROV.   [*After a pause*] My off-wheeler has gone lame for some reason. I noticed it yesterday when Peter was taking him to water.
VOITSKI.   You should have him reshod.
ASTROV.   I shall have to go around by the blacksmith's on my way home. It can't be avoided. [*He stands looking up at the map of Africa hanging on the wall*] I suppose it is roasting hot in Africa now.
VOITSKI.   Yes, I suppose it is.

MARINA *comes back carrying a tray on which are a glass of vodka and a piece of bread.*

MARINA.   Help yourself.

ASTROV *drinks.*

MARINA.   To your good health! [*She bows deeply*] Eat your bread with it.
ASTROV.   No, I like it so. And now, good-bye. [*To* MARINA] You needn't come out to see me off, nurse.

He goes out. SONIA *follows him with a candle to light him to the carriage.* MARINA *sits down in her armchair.*

VOITSKI.   [*Writing*] On the 2nd of February, twenty pounds of butter; on the 16th, twenty pounds of butter again. Buckwheat flour——

[*A pause. Bells are heard tinkling.*
MARINA.   He has gone.

[*A pause.*

SONIA *comes in and sets the candlestick on the table.*

SONIA.   He has gone.
VOITSKI.   [*Adding and writing*] Total, fifteen—twenty-five——

SONIA *sits down and begins to write.*

MARINA.   [*Yawning*] Oh, ho! The Lord have mercy.

TELEGIN *comes in on tiptoe, sits down near the door, and begins to tune his guitar.*

VOITSKI.   [*To* SONIA, *stroking her hair*] Oh, my child, I am so miserable; if you only knew how miserable I am!

SONIA.   What can we do? We must live our lives. [*A pause*] Yes, we shall live, Uncle Vanya. We shall live through the long procession of days before us, and through the long evenings; we shall patiently bear the trials that fate imposes on us; we shall work for others without rest, both now and when we are old; and when our last hour comes we shall meet it humbly, and there, beyond the grave, we shall say that we have suffered and wept, that our life was bitter, and God will have pity on us. Ah, then, dear, dear Uncle, we shall see that bright and beautiful life; we shall rejoice and look back upon our sorrow here; a tender smile—and—we shall rest. I have faith, Uncle, fervent, passionate faith. [SONIA *kneels down before her uncle and lays her head on his hands. She speaks in a weary voice*] We shall rest. [TELEGIN *plays softly on the guitar*] We shall rest. We shall hear the angels. We shall see heaven shining like a jewel. We shall see all evil and all our pain sink away in the great compassion that shall enfold the world. Our life will be as peaceful and tender and sweet as a caress. I have faith; I have faith. [*She wipes away her tears*] My poor, poor Uncle Vanya, you are crying! [*Weeping*] You have never known what happiness was, but wait, Uncle Vanya, wait! We shall rest. [*She embraces him*] We shall rest. [*The* WATCHMAN's *rattle is heard in the garden;* TELEGIN *plays softly;* MME. VOITSKAYA *writes something on the margin of her pamphlet;* MARINA *knits her stocking*] We shall rest.

The curtain slowly falls.

DOVER·THRIFT·EDITIONS

PLAYS

DOVER · THRIFT · EDITIONS

PLAYS

ELECTRA, Sophocles. 64pp. 28482-4

MISS JULIE, August Strindberg. 64pp. 27281-8

THE PLAYBOY OF THE WESTERN WORLD AND RIDERS TO THE SEA, J. M. Synge. 80pp. 27562-0

THE DUCHESS OF MALFI, John Webster. 96pp. 40660-1

THE IMPORTANCE OF BEING EARNEST, Oscar Wilde. 64pp. 26478-5

LADY WINDERMERE'S FAN, Oscar Wilde. 64pp. 40078-6

BOXED SETS

FAVORITE JANE AUSTEN NOVELS: *Pride and Prejudice, Sense and Sensibility* and *Persuasion* (Complete and Unabridged), Jane Austen. 800pp. 29748-9

BEST WORKS OF MARK TWAIN: Four Books, Dover. 624pp. 40226-6

EIGHT GREAT GREEK TRAGEDIES: Six Books, Dover. 480pp. 40203-7

FIVE GREAT ENGLISH ROMANTIC POETS, Dover. 496pp. 27893-X

FIVE GREAT PLAYS, Dover. 368pp. 27179-X

47 GREAT SHORT STORIES: Stories by Poe, Chekhov, Maupassant, Gogol, O. Henry, and Twain, Dover. 688pp. 27178-1

GREAT AFRICAN-AMERICAN WRITERS: Seven Books, Dover. 704pp. 29995-3

GREAT AMERICAN NOVELS, Dover. 720pp. 28665-7

GREAT ENGLISH NOVELS, Dover. 704pp. 28666-5

GREAT IRISH WRITERS: Five Books, Dover. 672pp. 29996-1

GREAT MODERN WRITERS: Five Books, Dover. 720pp. (Available in U.S. only.) 29458-7

GREAT WOMEN POETS: 4 Complete Books, Dover. 256pp. (Available in U.S. only.) 28388-7

MASTERPIECES OF RUSSIAN LITERATURE: Seven Books, Dover. 880pp. 40665-2

SEVEN GREAT ENGLISH VICTORIAN POETS: Seven Volumes, Dover. 592pp. 40204-5

SIX GREAT AMERICAN POETS: Poems by Poe, Dickinson, Whitman, Longfellow, Frost, and Millay, Dover. 512pp. (Available in U.S. only.) 27425-X

38 SHORT STORIES BY AMERICAN WOMEN WRITERS: Five Books, Dover. 512pp. 29459-5

26 GREAT TALES OF TERROR AND THE SUPERNATURAL, Dover. 608pp. (Available in U.S. only.) 27891-3